Fort Bend County Libraries

W9-BUM-824

WITHDRAWN

THE LEGEND OF
GRAVITY
A TALL BASKETBALL TALE

CHARLY PALMER

FARRAR STRAUS GIROUX
NEW YORK

I dedicate this book to my children, my grandchildren, and my wife, Dr. Karida Brown —C. P.

"All that I am, or hope to be, I owe to my angel mother." —Abraham Lincoln

Farrar Straus Giroux Books for Young Readers · An imprint of Macmillan Publishing Group, LLC · 120 Broadway, New York, NY 10271 · Copyright © 2022 by Charly L. Palmer · All rights reserved · Printed in China by RR Donnelley Asia Printing Solutions Ltd., Dongguan City, Guangdong Province · Designed by Jen Keenan and Neil Swaab · First edition, 2022 · mackids.com · Library of Congress Cataloging-in-Publication Data: Names: Palmer, Charly, writer, illustrator. Title: The legend of Gravity / written and illustrated by Charly Palmer. | Description: First edition. | New York : Farrar Straus Giroux Books for Young Readers, 2021. Audience: Ages 4-8 | Audience: Grades 2-3 | Summary: "A tall tale about a local basketball hero nicknamed Gravity"— Provided by publisher. | Identifiers: LCCN 2021005782 | ISBN 978-0-374-31328-9 (hardcover) | Subjects: CYAC: Basketball—Fiction. | Tall tales. | Classification: LCC PZ7.1.P3565 Le 2021 | DDC [E]—dc23 | LC record available at https://lccn.loc .gov/2021005782 · Our books may be purchased in bulk for promotional, educational, or business use. Please contact your local bookseller or the Macmillan Corporate and Premium Sales Department at (800) 221-7945 ext. 5442 or by email at MacmillanSpecialMarkets@macmillan.com.
10 9 8 7 6 5 4 3 2 1

I've heard you young folks talking about who is the best ballplayer to ever grace the court. Like that "King James" someone or other. He's not too shabby.

But have you ever heard of Gravity?

No, not *gravity*: the centripetal force
pulling us to the center of the earth.

I'm talking about GRAVITY: the greatest
ballplayer to ever lace up a pair of
sneakers.

Never heard of him? Well, pull up a chair and let me bend your ear for a minute with the legend of

GRAVITY.

One sunny afternoon in June, the twenty-ninth to be exact, Liquid was in the middle of one of his "lessons," trying to teach a new move to Sky High and Left 2 Right. Now, ole Liquid was talking, dribbling faster with his mouth than with the ball. He hated to be interrupted, but that's when this lanky, knobby-kneed, kind-of-awkward new kid strolled onto the playground court.

He wore baggy shorts hanging down to his knees.
And he had waves so tight it would make you seasick.

He asked if he might join us
in a three-on-three.

Liquid, a bit fed up with the audacious interruption, tossed the ball at the new kid. The boy caught it as though it were an intended pass rather than an outright assault.

He spun it on his finger,

dribbled it between his legs,

then proceeded to run circles
around Left 2 Right and Liquid and . . .

. . . leaped gracefully into the air over Sky High.

Now, Sky High wasn't called Sky High for nothing. When he jumped, he looked like he could touch the clouds. But this new kid cleared Sky, flipped the ball behind his own back, through his legs, and kept going.

Everyone stood there for a moment with their mouths hanging wide open. When he snapped out of it, Sky sputtered, "He's on my team." Since the ball we were playing with belonged to Sky, no one bothered to argue.

"What's your playground name, man?" I asked.
"I don't have one," said the boy.
"Everybody needs a street name," said Liquid.

"Why don't we call him Orbit because he jumped into space?" said Sky High.

"And we call him Left 2 Right because you never know where he's going."

"They call me Liquid because I'm so smooth."

LIQUID

LEFT 2 RIGHT

SKY HIGH

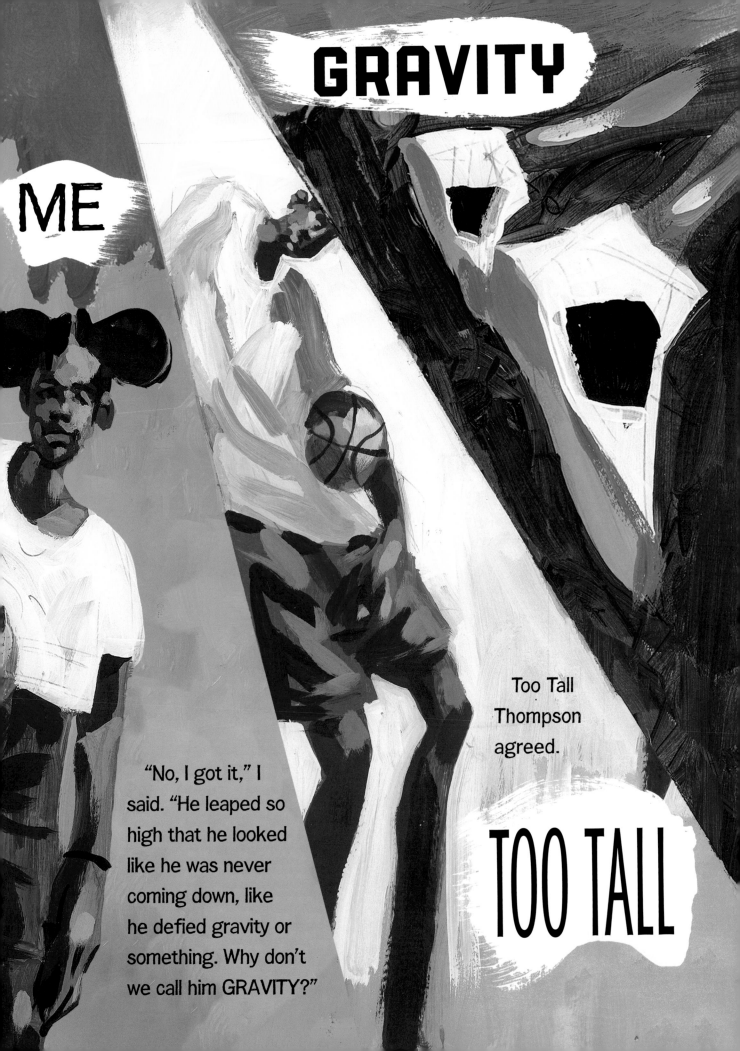

GRAVITY

ME

Too Tall
Thompson
agreed.

"No, I got it," I
said. "He leaped so
high that he looked
like he was never
coming down, like
he defied gravity or
something. Why don't
we call him GRAVITY?"

TOO TALL

And that's how Gravity joined our playground team, the Eagles.

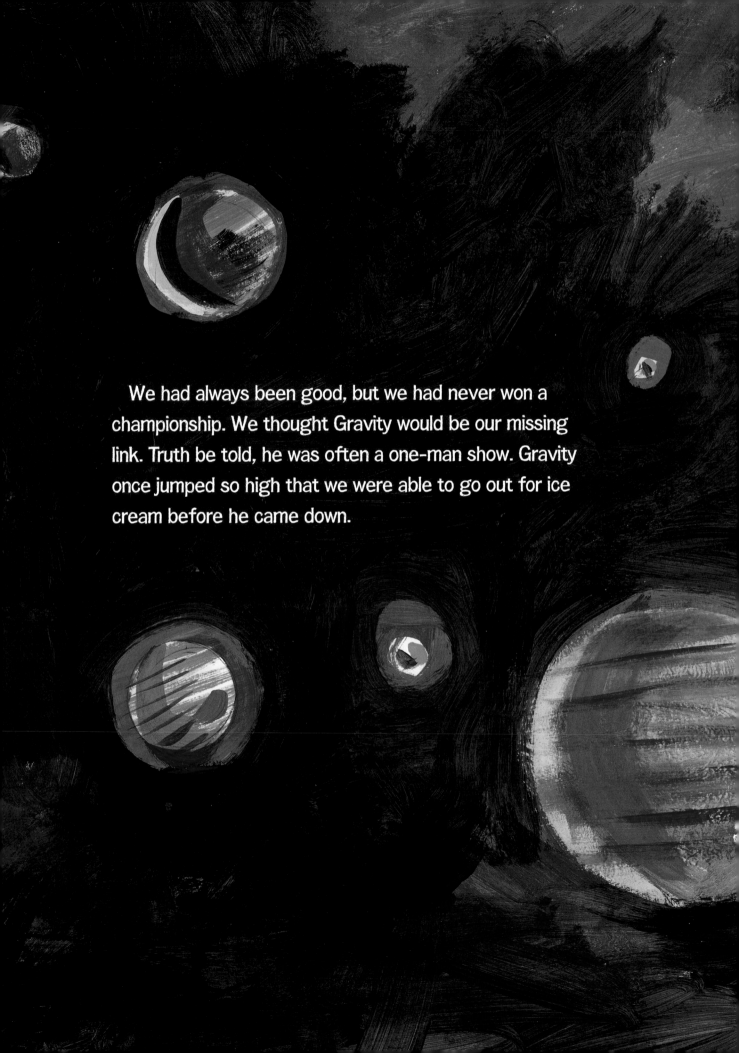

We had always been good, but we had never won a championship. We thought Gravity would be our missing link. Truth be told, he was often a one-man show. Gravity once jumped so high that we were able to go out for ice cream before he came down.

Ballers from across the city started coming around, trying to challenge Gravity. In one game, he scored 150 points. Oh, you're not impressed? You should be. Gravity scored all those points in the first quarter. He left the game early, something to do with babysitting his sister.

That summer, Gravity had us believing that no team, nowhere, could beat us.

We ruled the blacktop courts in the Hillside projects, where we lived. We played all day and all night—and even after church on Sundays. Some days, we walked, rode bikes, or took the bus so we could go to other courts in other neighborhoods and beat other teams.

Our winning streak got longer as the summer was coming to an end. And everyone was looking forward to the "Best of the Best," Milwaukee's biggest and baddest pickup basketball tournament. Although we had dreams of winning it one day, we never believed we could. Not until we had Gravity.

The weekend before the Best of the Best, we had a team meeting to work out a strategy. In five seconds flat, we agreed our only hope was getting the ball to Gravity and letting him do the rest.

And sure enough, Gravity was amazing.

Dribbling behind his back,
between his legs,
and even off the backboard.

Gravity made plays no one had ever
seen before.

He ran the offense like magic,

lobbing passes from out of nowhere . . .

and leaving us shocked
to find the ball in our
hands for an easy layup.

He was turning every game into a highlight video.

Gravity's legend grew from Friday to Saturday as we plowed down one team after another. Thanks to Gravity, we made it all the way to the finals on Sunday.

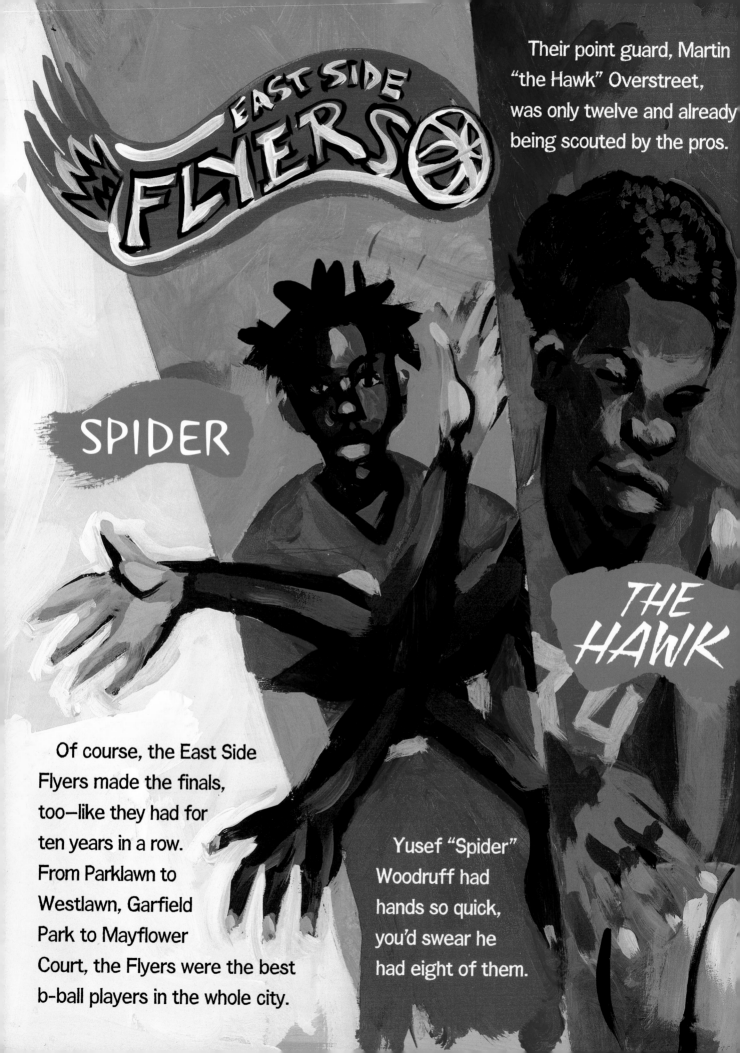

EAST SIDE FLYERS

Their point guard, Martin "the Hawk" Overstreet, was only twelve and already being scouted by the pros.

SPIDER

THE HAWK

Of course, the East Side Flyers made the finals, too—like they had for ten years in a row. From Parklawn to Westlawn, Garfield Park to Mayflower Court, the Flyers were the best b-ball players in the whole city.

Yusef "Spider" Woodruff had hands so quick, you'd swear he had eight of them.

And then there was Benny "the Jet" Street. He was the Flyers' one-man fast-break machine.

We once watched Richard "Deep Water" Brown put away 14 threes in a single half.

DEEP WATER

Their center, Lyle "the Giant" Harris, stood six feet seven inches tall.

THE JET

THE GIANT

On game day, it seemed the whole city had come to watch. The Flyers formed a circle, piled their hands on top of one another, and said,

"One, two, three, VICTORY!"

We were so intimidated, we decided to do the same. So we huddled up on the sideline and said the obvious:

"One, two, three, GRAVITY!"

At first, the Flyers matched us point for point.

As I went for a layup, Lyle the Giant slapped my shot in the opposite direction, and the Jet scored two points with a short jumper.

On our next trip down the court, Left 2 Right tried to fake a pass to me.

But the Spider stole the ball and scoop-passed it to the Jet for another jumper that dropped through the net with a

swish.

The next time we got the ball, Gravity decided to take control.
When the Flyers surrounded him on defense, Gravity zipped a pass
to Sky High, who drove to the basket but ran straight into the Hawk.
The referee whistled a foul charge—against us!

By halftime, we were tied 42 to
42, and Gravity was out of breath—
exhausted. We needed a different
strategy to win.

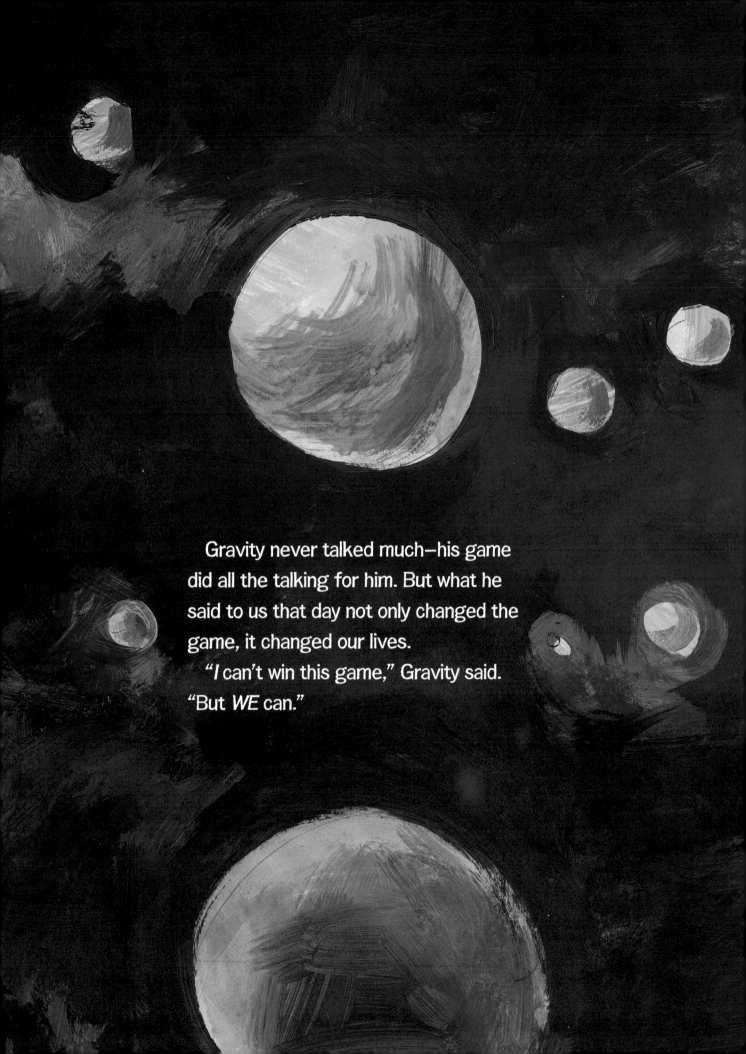

Gravity never talked much—his game
did all the talking for him. But what he
said to us that day not only changed the
game, it changed our lives.

"*I* can't win this game," Gravity said.
"But *WE* can."

He looked at Liquid and said, "Man, you flow like water. It's time for you to turn on the tap full blast!"

Gravity moved to Sky High. "You have hops like no other guy on the court. Why aren't you flying to the basket?"

"Left 2 Right, with your killer crossover dribble, people can't tell if you're coming or going.
"And you, Too Tall, just get in the way!"

Finally, he focused on me. Now, I'd never had a nickname, but when Gravity said, "I'ma call you . . . Butta! You got flava, so we need you to melt into the backcourt and spread the defense," something inside of me got unstuck.

This time, our team circled up, piled our hands on top of one another, and yelled in unison,

"One, two, three, TEAM!!!!"

By tip-off, Gravity had us hyped. The Flyers might
as well have surrendered right then and there.

I caught the tip-off.

And as I dribbled up the court, I whispered to myself,
"Get out the way, or get served by Butta."
The Flyers never knew what hit them.

For the first time, Sky High, Left 2 Right, Liquid,
Too Tall, Butta, and, of course, Gravity played as one.

We confused the Flyers by
constantly changing our defense.

We ran man-to-man coverage,

then switched to the two-three-two zone,

and then shifted to our triangle, trapping defense.

With less than two minutes left, our shots started falling like a hard summer rain. Suddenly we were unstoppable, hitting three-pointers, jump hooks, and high-arching fade-away jumpers that made the crowd roar. Our defense shut down their offense for good.

When the final buzzer sounded, everyone was stunned by the scoreboard. We had beaten the Flyers by 17 points!

There was no doubt that Gravity was the most valuable player that day, maybe ever. But he insisted that we all share the championship trophy, passing it from teammate to teammate.

Twenty-five years later, we still do.

AUTHOR'S NOTE

I would like to thank all who inspired this story. That includes unsung basketball greats who never made it to the NBA but left a lasting impression on those who witnessed their incredible feats and heard their amazing stories and are still sharing them with the world. This book is dedicated to streetball legends including Ed "Booger" Smith, Rick "Pee-Wee" Kirkland, Earl "the Goat" Manigault, Demetrius "Hook" Mitchell, and Joe "the Destroyer" Hammond.

I would like to thank Dorothea Taylor, who helped develop the initial story of Gravity; Ida T. Harris, who helped with the initial editing; and Lyle V. Harris, a journalist and native Brooklynite, for sharing his basketball knowledge, which was extremely helpful. And Sanchez Johnson for helping with the initial sketches.

I also dedicate this book to Richard "Deep Water" Brown. Your greatness goes beyond the courts. And to one of Milwaukee's streetball legends, Albert "Spoony" Hall, who like many great players never got a chance to shine in an arena, but shined on the outside courts all over the world. Finally, to Jordan Smith (Gravity's inspiration). When we gathered for the photo shoot and I first saw you, I knew that you had to be my muse. Jordan, I say, you are a star.

Now, when you hear about players like Gravity, please bear in mind that these stories were passed along by word of mouth. The more often they're told, the more they become hearsay. Whenever a story begins, "I heard that . . . blah, blah, blah," I know right away they only heard what I saw with my own eyes. In my youth, nobody had mobile phones with cameras, so pictures and videos from that time are rare. Like unicorns and mermaids, people claim to have seen these fantastic creatures. But this is no fantasy, and that's why I wrote this story about what happened that day on the blacktop in Milwaukee, Wisconsin.